Scion®

Blood
For Blood

Scion®

BLOOD FOR BLOOD

Ron **MARZ**
WRITER

Jim **CHEUNG**
PENCILER

Don **HILLSMAN II**
INKER

Caesar **RODRIGUEZ** (CHAPTERS 8-10)

Justin **PONSOR** (CHAPTERS 11, 13-14)
COLORISTS

CHAPTER 12

Andrea **DI VITO** · PENCILER
Rob **HUNTER** · INKER
Paul **MOUNTS** · COLORIST

CROSSGEN CHRONICLES #2

George **PÉREZ** · PENCILER
Dennis **JENSEN** with
Rick **MAGYAR** · CG INKERS
Laura **MARTIN** · COLORIST

Dave **LANPHEAR** and Troy **PETERI**
LETTERERS

CrossGeneration Comics   Oldsmar, Florida

BLOOD FOR BLOOD
features Chapters 8 - 14 and
CrossGen Chronicles #2
of the ongoing series
SCION

Avalon is actually two worlds: one, a medieval façade that maintains a connection with the planet's feudal past; the other, the fabulous technology hidden beneath that veneer. Science has enabled the creation of everything from hovercraft that skim the sea's surface, to the diversity of life-forms known as the Lesser Races that were spawned through genetic manipulation.

Two great dynasties, the Herons of the West and the Ravens of the East, have ruled Avalon for centuries. Their long-standing hatreds run deep and the kingdoms warred for centuries until a fragile truce was forged. That truce was shattered by a young Heron prince named Ethan. After being branded with a sigil whose power he could neither understand nor control, Ethan scarred the Raven heir to the throne, Bron, during the annual tournament of ritual combat that had replaced open warfare.

Ethan surrendered himself to the Ravens, but was soon freed from his imprisonment by a woman named Ashleigh, who wanted Ethan to join the Underground's cause of freedom for the Lesser Races. Ethan declined her offer and returned home as the clouds of war gathered on the horizon.

The initial battle was met upon the Western shore at Point Korday, Ethan fighting at the side of his brothers, Kai and Artor, and sister, Ylena. Ultimate victory belonged to the Herons, but at a terrible price. Artor, heir to the throne, was brutally slain by Bron. As Artor was laid to rest in the family crypt, a man calling himself Bernd Rechts appeared and offered his services as war advisor. Rechts showed great interest in Ethan's sigil, but could not dissuade the young prince from departing for the East so he could avenge his brother's death.

HE PUSHED THE HERONS AND RAVENS TOWARD PEACE MORE THAN A CENTURY AGO. AND NOW WE'RE AT WAR AGAIN...

WHOKT

...BECAUSE OF *ME.*

ETHAN, SOMETIMES YOUR DESTINY CHOOSES *YOU,* RATHER THAN YOU CHOOSING IT. DON'T BLAME YOURSELF FOR THINGS BEYOND YOUR CONTROL.

LIKE THE WAR?

LIKE MY BROTHER'S MURDER?

THERE'S NO NEED TO SPARE MY FEELINGS, SKINK. WE'VE KNOWN EACH OTHER TOO LONG.

THE TRUTH IS NONE OF THIS WOULD'VE HAPPENED IF *I* HADN'T CAUSED IT...

...IF I HADN'T BEEN BRANDED WITH THIS SIGIL.

MOST PEOPLE *CELEBRATE* ON THEIR BIRTHDAYS.

I SET TWO KINGDOMS TO WAR.

THEY FORGED ME THE SWORD OF THE MAN WHO BROUGHT THE HERON-RAVEN WAR TO AN END.

AND I HAVE EVERY INTENTION OF USING IT TO *KILL* A RAVEN PRINCE.

NO ONE WOULD ARGUE YOUR VOW TO AVENGE ARTOR'S DEATH, ETHAN. IT'S A MATTER OF HONOR.

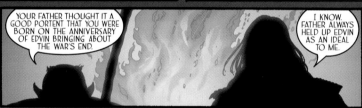

YOUR FATHER THOUGHT IT A GOOD PORTENT THAT YOU WERE BORN ON THE ANNIVERSARY OF EDVIN BRINGING ABOUT THE WAR'S END.

I KNOW. FATHER ALWAYS HELD UP EDVIN AS AN IDEAL TO ME.

BUT I DON'T THINK I'VE DONE A VERY GOOD JOB OF LIVING UP TO HIS LEGACY.

EDVIN WAS ADMIRAL OF THE HERON FLEET...

...LOYAL BROTHER TO THE KING...

...THE *PEACE MAKER*...

...HOW AM I SUPPOSED TO FIND A RAVEN FLEET THAT SEEMS DETERMINED TO HIDE FROM US?

I'VE NO TASTE FOR THIS CAT AND MOUSE GAME, GRUM. I BEGIN TO WONDER IF WE'RE THE HUNTER OR THE HUNTED.

SIRE, DISPATCHES HAVE ARRIVED.

THE WEATHER'S BLOWING IN FROM THE NORTH AND IS EXPECTED TO WORSEN.

AYE, WHY SHOULDN'T IT? NOTHING *ELSE* ABOUT THIS VOYAGE HAS GONE IN OUR FAVOR.

AND ALL SO WE CAN BUTCHER MEN SIMPLY BECAUSE THEY WERE BORN ON THE FAR SIDE OF THE SEA.

WE HERONS AND RAVENS HAVE BEEN AT EACH OTHER'S THROATS FOR SO LONG WE DON'T EVEN REMEMBER WHY WE FIGHT. *FOOLS,* ALL OF US, FOOLS.

BUT IT'S NOT MY PLACE TO GAINSAY MY KINGDOM OR MY KING, EVEN WHEN IT'S MY BROTHER WHO SITS ON THE THRONE.

ADMIRAL EDVIN!

SIGHTING TO PORT!

FINALLY.

GLASS!

STEADY ON, HELM. I WANT TO BE WITHIN *SPITTING DISTANCE* OF THAT BASTARD ALEXI'S FLAGSHIP BEFORE WE UNLEASH OUR BATTERIES.

WHAT OF THE STORM, ADMIRAL?

IT'LL BE ON TOP OF US SOON, AND IT'S WORSENING. COULD EVEN BE BLOWING UP INTO A NORTHERN GALE.

AND WHAT WOULD YOU LIKE ME TO *DO* ABOUT IT, HELMSMAN? LET NATURE DO WHAT SHE WILL...

"...WE'VE GOT MORE IMMEDIATE CONCERNS."

ONLY THE FIRST BLOW, GENTLEMEN.

THEY'LL TRY TO CHASE US DOWN AND LOOSE A BROADSIDE. COME ABOUT AND TELL THE GUN DECKS TO RELOAD.

HEEL US OVER! STARBOARD GUNS RELOAD!

Oh, no...

ADMIRAL, THEY'RE NOT LAYING OVER!

THEY MEAN TO *RAM* US!

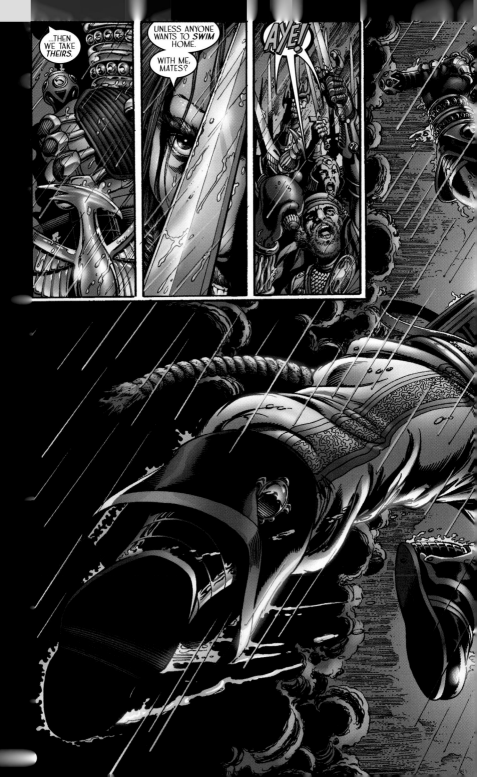

HRRK!

CHANG

SPLIT YOU FROM STEM TO STERN, HERON DOG! *SPLIT YOU*—

CHOKT

EDVIN...

...I'M *TRULY* HAPPY TO SEE YOU ALIVE.

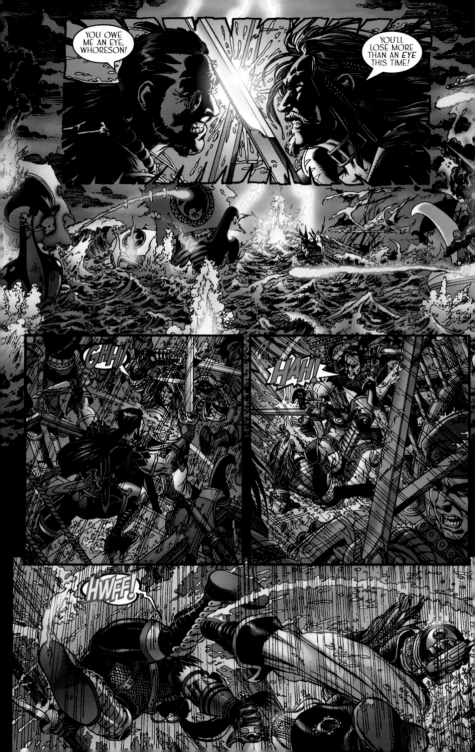

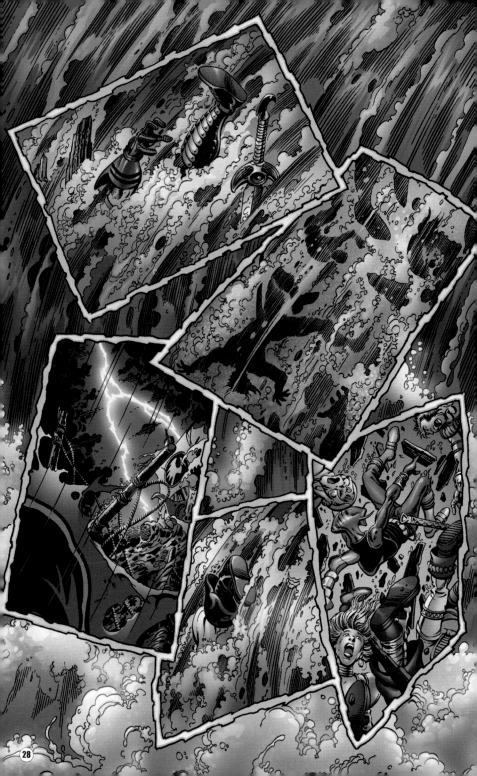

whuh

whur'm...

...WHERE AM I? SOME... ISLAND?

AND HOW DID I GET HERE? I DON'T REMEMBER ANYTHING EXCEPT... THE WATER.

THE WATER AND EDVIN.

MY CREW.

NO SIGN OF THE FLEET...

...BUT I *CAN'T* BE THE ONLY ONE WHO SURVIVED THE STORM. THERE MUST BE SOMEONE ELSE...

→NNH←

→NH←

→NH←

→GH←

THIS...

SKAAASH

OUR ANCESTOR WAS A FOOL.

ALEXI FORGED THE PEACE WITH THE HERONS, INITIATED THE RITUAL COMBAT TO TAKE THE WAR'S PLACE, BUILT THE ARENA ON THE TOURNAMENT ISLE.

AND WE PRESERVE HIS BLADE LIKE AN HONORED TROPHY.

IS THAT WHAT YOU BELIEVE, MY SON?

WE'D HAVE WIPED THE HERONS FROM THE FACE OF AVALON *LONG AGO* IF NOT FOR ALEXI'S WEAKNESS!

PERHAPS WHAT YOU DEEM WEAKNESS WAS NECESSITY. A WAY TO PRESERVE A KINGDOM WHOSE RESOURCES HAD BEEN EXHAUSTED BY DECADE UPON DECADE OF WAR.

WHILE THE TRUCE HELD, OUR KINGDOM TENDED ITS WOUNDS. WE GREW STRONG. AND NOW WE MAKE WAR AGAIN.

IS IT TRULY EDVIN'S PEACE THAT VEXES YOU, BRON? OR IS IT PERHAPS THE *SCAR* YOU BEAR?

THE WESTERN WHELP WILL PAY FOR HIS TREACHERY! I'LL PUT THIS BLADE TO ITS *PROPER* USE, FATHER, AND OPEN ETHAN'S THROAT AS I DID HIS BROTHER'S!

BRON, YOU ARE MY ELDEST. YOU ARE TO FOLLOW ME TO THE THRONE ONE DAY...

...IF YOU LEARN TO CONTROL YOURSELF. IF YOU MEAN TO BE KING, YOU MUST BE MASTER OF YOUR ANGER, NOT LET IT MASTER YOU.

YOUR TEMPER DOES NOT BEFIT ONE OF RAVEN NOBLE BLOOD. AND IT WILL NOT SIT WELL ON THE HEAD THAT WEARS THE CROWN.

I ADVISE YOU TO THINK ON THESE THINGS, MY SON.

HAVE A SERVANT REMOVE THE MESS YOU MADE...

...BUT KNOW THERE WON'T ALWAYS BE SOMEONE TO CLEAN UP AFTER YOU.

YES, FATHER.

KEEP LOOKING DOWN YOUR NOSE AT ME, OLD MAN...

...YOU'LL NEVER SEE ME BEHIND YOU.

ANYTHING?

NORTH.

FATHER'S NOT GOING TO BE PLEASED WHEN HE FINDS WE'VE BOTH LEFT THE KEEP FOR SOMETHING LIKE *THIS* AT A TIME OF WAR.

WELL IT'S NOT *FATHER'S* SLAVE WHO ESCAPED, *IS IT,* KORT?

AN AGENT OF THE UNDERGROUND, RIGHT IN MY OWN CHAMBERS. WHO KNOWS WHAT SECRETS HE'S CARRYING BACK TO THEM.

I WON'T BE SEEN AS A FOOL WHO COULDN'T EVEN COMMAND THE OBEDIENCE OF HIS OWN SLAVE.

WE DON'T GO HOME UNTIL HE'S *SPITTED* ON MY BLADE, LITTLE BROTHER. AND IF HE LEADS US TO THE UNDERGROUND'S ENCLAVE...

KRAKOOM

...SO MUCH THE *BETTER.*

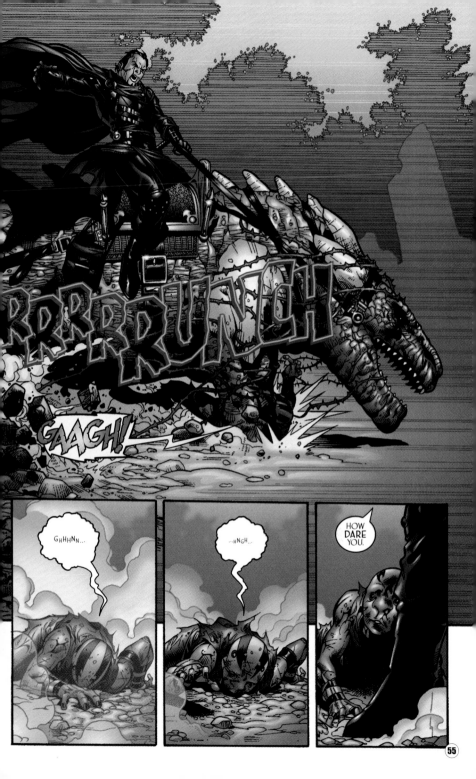

FILTH.

SHUK

EASY, WASN'T IT?

BUT THEN YOU NEVER FOUND *MURDER* TERRIBLY DIFFICULT ANYWAY.

MY MOUNT! WHO DID THIS?! HOW?!

FIRST AND LAST WARNING, BRON.

DON'T COME HERE AGAIN.

OR WE'LL KILL YOU.

WHAT GOES ON HERE, SISTER?!

SNAP!

ANSWER ME, ASHLEIGH.

ASHLEIGH?

"WE'RE AT WAR FOR THE FIRST TIME IN TWO CENTURIES, WE GET ROUTED AND DRIVEN FROM THE ENEMY'S SHORES..."

...AND YOU TWO CAN'T FIND ANYTHING BETTER TO DO THAN RIDE OFF AFTER AN ESCAPED SLAVE!

I EXPECT SOMETHING LIKE THIS FROM YOU, BRON, BUT I THOUGHT YOU KNEW BETTER, KORT. IT'S TIME YOU STOPPED BEING SWEPT UP BY YOUR BROTHER'S FITS OF TEMPER.

BY OUR *ANCESTORS*, BRON, YOU'RE NEXT IN LINE FOR THE THRONE. THIS BEHAVIOR ONLY EXACERBATES MY CONCERNS OVER YOUR READINESS TO SUCCEED ME ONE DAY.

NOW THAT YOUR LITTLE ADVENTURE'S CONCLUDED, DID ANYTHING USEFUL COME OF IT?

NO, FATHER...

...NOTHING.

NO, OF COURSE NOT.

I WANT YOU BOTH TO MEET SOMEONE WHO ARRIVED WHILE YOU WERE GONE ON YOUR FOOL'S ERRAND. SOMEONE WHO'S GOING TO BE QUITE USEFUL TO US.

SHUT DOWN, THE SHORE'S JUST AHEAD.

I HAVE TO BE HONEST, ETHAN. I CAN'T SAY I'M OVERJOYED AT BEING BACK IN EASTERN LANDS.

I DON'T THINK I'VE *EVER* SEEN YOU OVERJOYED, SKINK.

BUT I'VE SWORN TO REPAY BRON IN KIND FOR ARTOR'S MURDER, AND I DON'T THINK HE'S ABOUT TO COME TO *US*.

WE AT LEAST NEED SOMEPLACE TO START LOOKING. WHEN ASHLEIGH GAVE THIS TO ME, SHE SAID IT WOULD LEAD ME TO HER.

LET'S FIND OUT.

DEET

THERE, CERTAINLY.

ETHAN SHOULD'VE REACHED THE EASTERN SHORE BY NOW ASSUMING THE SEA CROSSING WENT WELL.

BUT HE WON'T BE CONTACTING US FOR FEAR OF BEING FOUND OUT BY RAVEN COMMUNICATION SWEEPERS.

KAI, I WANT ARTOR'S DEATH AVENGED AS MUCH AS ANYONE, BUT I'M AFRAID ETHAN'S BEEN DRIVEN TO THIS BY THE GUILT HE'S FEELING.

ETHAN BLAMES HIMSELF FOR THE WAR, HE BLAMES HIMSELF FOR ARTOR'S DEATH. HE SEES AVENGING ARTOR AS HIS PENANCE...

...AND IF HE PLACES HIMSELF IN HARM'S WAY WHILE HE DOES IT, I THINK HE'S CONVINCED HIMSELF HE DESERVES IT.

EVEN IF ETHAN DOES FIND BRON, DO YOU THINK HE STANDS A CHANCE OF DEFEATING HIM?

SPLIP

THERE AREN'T MANY FIERCER OPPONENTS THAN BRON ON ALL AVALON. WE HAVE A DEAD BROTHER TO PROVE IT.

BUT THAT MARK ON ETHAN'S ARM, *WHATEVER* IT IS, MAKES HIM SOMETHING SPECIAL.

EVEN SO, I WORRY FOR HIM.

I KNOW HE'S A MAN NOW, BUT I'LL ALWAYS THINK OF HIM AS MY LITTLE BROTHER.

YES, THAT. A CURIOUS OCCURENCE INDEED. ONE I HOPE TO BE ABLE TO INVESTIGATE UPON ETHAN'S SAFE RETURN.

I'VE TAKEN ENOUGH OF YOUR TIME ALREADY. I'M SURE YOU HAVE OTHER MATTERS TO ATTEND TO, AS DO I. IF YOU'LL EXCUSE ME.

CERTAINLY.

DO YOU TRUST HIM?

FATHER SEEMS TO...

...I'M NOT QUITE SO CERTAIN. MAYBE RECHTS DID COME TO OUR KINGDOM ONLY TO OFFER HIS SERVICES AS A STRATEGIST, BUT I SUSPECT HE HAS SOME OTHER AGENDA...

...AT LEAST WHERE ETHAN'S CONCERNED.

WE'VE BEEN WORRIED ABOUT ETHAN'S WELFARE. IT'S POSSIBLE HE'S SAFER WHERE HE IS...

"...AWAY FROM HERE."

NO ONE IN THE EAST EXPECTS ME TO BE HERE...

...BUT THERE'S NO SENSE IN ADVERTISING OURSELVES.

I DOUBT WE'LL BE RECOGNIZED, BUT BEST NOT TO TAKE ANY CHANCES.

READY, SKINK?

I'VE FOLLOWED YOU SINCE BEFORE YOU COULD WALK, ETHAN.

LEAD ON.

ETHAN!
THERE AT THE
BACK OF THE
DAIS...

"...EXETER."

BUT...

...BUT I *KILLED* HIM! HE SHOULD BE *DEAD!*

ETHAN! KEEP YOUR VOICE *DOWN!*

I DON'T KNOW HOW, BUT HE'S OBVIOUSLY *NOT* DEAD.

HE'S PROBABLY HERE MAKING SURE NO ONE WITH A PRICE ON THEIR HEAD TRIES TO ESCAPE BY JOINING THE MILITARY. HE *CAN'T* BE LOOKING FOR US...

"...HE COULDN'T EVEN KNOW WE'RE BACK IN EASTERN LANDS."

YOU'RE RIGHT. LET'S JUST GET THIS OVER WITH.

WHILE THE REST OF THE TOWN IS GAWKING AT THE SOLDIERS WE CAN GET WHAT WE CAME FOR.

THERE'S THE STABLE.

I DIDN'T LIKE STEALING THAT BOAT LAST TIME WE WERE IN THE EAST. I'M NOT ENTIRELY COMFORTABLE WITH *THIS*, EITHER.

THERE'S NOT REALLY ANOTHER CHOICE, ETHAN, IS THERE? IF WE'RE GOING TO COVER ANY GROUND, WE NEED MOUNTS.

I KNOW...

...BUT MY PARENTS DIDN'T RAISE ME TO BE A THIEF. I LEARNED MY LESSON WHEN MY FATHER CAUGHT ME FILCHING PASTRIES FROM THE SERVANTS' LARDER.

DO YOU REMEMBER *THAT?* I WAS SCRUBBING KITCHEN POTS FOR A MONTH.

BDEEP

I JUST WANT TO DO THIS AS QUICKLY AS POSSIBLE AND GET...

...OUT OF HERE.

ETHAN! WHERE ARE WE HEADED?!

WE FOLLOW THE MAP, SKINK...

...NORTH!

THIS IS THE PLACE...

...BUT THERE'S NOTHING HERE. TWO DAYS' RIDE AND NOTHING BUT RUINS.

NO SIGN OF ASHLEIGH, NO SIGN OF THE UNDERGROUND.

SINCE WE'RE *HERE*, I MIGHT AS WELL HAVE A LOOK AROUND.

BE CAREFUL, ETHAN. SOMETHING FEELS...WRONG... ABOUT THIS PLACE.

ALL MAY NOT BE AS IT APPEARS.

I WONDER WHAT THESE RUINS *WERE*, OUT IN THE MIDDLE OF NOWHERE LIKE THIS.

A BETTER VANTAGE POINT COULDN'T HURT...

...THOUGH I DOUBT THERE'S ANYTHING TO SEE.

NOTHING AT ALL. JUST CRUMBLING BUILDINGS AND A STAIRCASE LEADING NOWHERE.

MAYBE THERE NEVER *WAS* ANYTHING MORE, AND ASHLEIGH WAS JUST—

UHH?

WHAT WAS *THAT?*

SOME KIND OF—

ASHLEIGH?

SHE GAVE ME *THIS...*

...AND TOLD ME IT WOULD LEAD ME TO HER.

IF ASHLEIGH TRUSTS YOU ENOUGH TO SEND YOU HERE, THEN YOU'RE WELCOME AMONG US.

APOLOGIES FOR THE HARSH RECEPTION...

...BUT WE CAN'T BE TOO CAREFUL.

Oh.

SORRY, IT'S...

...THE SWORD'S A LONG STORY.

I'M STILL NOT ENTIRELY SURE ABOUT IT.

"...COMPARED TO THE SLAVERY THEY'VE LIVED WITH SINCE BIRTH.

"THE UNDERGROUND INTENDS TO WIN FREEDOM FOR ALL LESSER RACES BY WHATEVER MEANS NECESSARY. THE SANCTUARY'S A *START*..."

...IT PROVES SUCH A THING IS POSSIBLE.

ETHAN, THERE'S SOMEONE YOU SHOULD MEET.

ANNIL AND HER SON ESCAPED THEIR SERVITUDE AND WERE ABLE TO REACH THE SANCTUARY A FEW WEEKS AGO. HER HUSBAND, THE CHILD'S FATHER, WAS TO HAVE JOINED THEM HERE...

...BUT HE WAS SLAIN BY PRINCE BRON, CUT DOWN AT THE FOOT OF THE STEPS OUTSIDE BEFORE WE COULD DO ANYTHING TO STOP IT. HE'D BEEN BRON'S PERSONAL SERVANT FOR YEARS.

IT'S ONE OF *THEM*. MAKE IT GO AWAY.

YOU SHOULD BE *ASHAMED* COMING TO THIS PLACE! YOUR KIND HAS NO RIGHT HERE!

WHAT?

MAMA...

SHHH, IT'S ALL RIGHT. WE'RE SAFE NOW.

BUT...

...BUT I'M NOT GOING TO HURT YOU. YOU DON'T HAVE TO BE AFRAID OF—

THE EAST'S LESSER RACES *LEARN* TO FEAR HUMANS. OR WE TEND NOT TO LIVE VERY LONG.

THE ONLY HUMAN WE'VE COME TO TRUST IS ASHLEIGH.

WHERE *IS* ASHLEIGH? I'D LIKE TO SEE HER.

SHE'S FAIRLY PRIVATE. KEEPS TO HERSELF QUITE A BIT.

IT'S NOT FOR ME TO TELL YOU MORE.

SHE'S NOT HERE, I DON'T KNOW WHEN SHE *WILL* BE HERE.

THIS IS A SANCTUARY. I WON'T TURN YOU OUT, BUT I DON'T KNOW HOW WELCOME YOU'LL BE MADE TO FEEL IF YOU'RE NOT HERE TO SUPPORT OUR CAUSE.

NO, I UNDERSTAND.

WE'LL GO.

THANK YOU, THAT'S VERY KIND.

I WANT YOU TO KNOW I'M NOT TURNING MY BACK ON THE UNDERGROUND. I *DO* WANT TO HELP YOU.

BUT I SWORE TO MY FAMILY THAT I'D AVENGE MY BROTHER. YOU UNDERSTAND THAT, DON'T YOU?

WE CAN'T SPARE MUCH IN THE WAY OF SUPPLIES, BUT WE SHOULD BE ABLE TO SCRAPE UP SOMETHING FOR YOU AND YOUR MOUNTS.

OF COURSE...

...I UNDERSTAND PERFECTLY.

THAT DIDN'T ACCOMPLISH *ANYTHING* EXCEPT ALIENATING ME FROM THE UNDERGROUND.

I'M NOT SURE WHAT YOUR *NEW* PLAN OF ACTION IS GOING TO ACCOMPLISH EITHER, ETHAN. EXCEPT GETTING YOU KILLED.

RIDING INTO THE RAVEN CAPITAL AND TRYING TO SNEAK INTO THE KEEP DOESN'T STRIKE ME AS THE WISEST COURSE.

I'M PERFECTLY WILLING TO CONSIDER ALTERNATIVES, SKINK. THERE JUST *AREN'T* ANY.

I DON'T HAVE A WAY OF LURING BRON SOMEPLACE THAT WOULD FAVOR *ME*, SO I HAVE TO GO TO HIM.

HERE... ...THIS LOOKS TO BE AS GOOD A PLACE AS ANY TO CAMP.

I CAME TO SLAY BRON, THAT'S WHAT I'M GOING TO DO. AFTER THAT...

...AFTER THAT, I WISH I KNEW.

WHEN YOU WERE BRANDED WITH THE SIGIL, THE PATH OF YOUR LIFE CHANGED, ETHAN. IT'S NOT POSSIBLE FOR YOU TO KNOW WHAT YOUR FUTURE HOLDS.

I CAN'T TELL YOUR DESTINY.

I'LL GATHER WOOD FOR A FIRE. THERE'S A CHILL ROLLING IN.

I'LL SEE TO OUR MOUNTS.

I UNDERSTAND YOU *DIED*, ARTOR. YOU DIED BECAUSE OF *ME*.

IF I HADN'T SET ALL THESE THINGS INTO MOTION, YOU NEVER WOULD'VE BEEN *ON* THAT BATTLEFIELD.

I'M SO SORRY.

I DIDN'T COME TO DWELL ON THE THINGS THAT CAN'T BE CHANGED, ETHAN.

I'VE TOLD YOU MY TIME IS SHORT. WE NEED TO SPEAK OF THE THINGS THAT ARE YET TO BE.

WE NEED TO SPEAK OF THE FUTURE.

YOU MEAN THE *WAR?*

YES AND NO. A GREATER DESTINY AWAITS YOU, LITTLE BROTHER...

...BECAUSE OF THIS.

UP UNTIL NOW, THE ONLY THING THE SIGIL'S DONE IS CAUSE *SUFFERING*. I'M LEARNING WHAT IT'S CAPABLE OF...

...OR AT LEAST WHAT IT'S BEEN CAPABLE OF SO FAR. BUT I *STILL* HAVE NO IDEA WHAT IT IS OR HOW I *GOT* IT.

IS THAT WHY YOU'RE HERE? CAN YOU TELL ME WHAT IT MEANS?

THE SIGIL IS NOT A RANDOM THING, ETHAN. YOU WERE *CHOSEN* TO RECEIVE IT. YOU...

...*AND* OTHERS.

IT CAN BE A GREAT BOON FOR THOSE ABLE TO BEAR ITS WEIGHT, A KEY TO BECOMING MORE THAN THEY IMAGINE POSSIBLE.

THE SIGIL'S POWER GOES FAR BEYOND SIMPLY PUTTING A SWORD IN YOUR HAND OR HEALING YOUR WOUNDS. YOU WILL COME TO UNDERSTAND *ALL* THIS.

IN TIME YOU MAY BE CALLED TO FIGHT IN A GREAT BATTLE. IF THAT DAY ARRIVES, YOU MUST BE PREPARED...

...YOU MUST BE THE *WARRIOR* THE SIGIL CAN MAKE OF YOU.

WHAT KIND OF BATTLE?

I NEED TO KNOW *MORE*, ARTOR.

WHO GAVE ME THE SIGIL? WHAT DO THEY WANT?

I CANNOT PROVIDE YOU WITH ANSWERS, ETHAN.

I CAN ONLY HELP YOU LEARN WHAT QUESTIONS TO ASK.

MY TIME DRAWS TO A CLOSE...

...AND I'VE ALREADY SAID MORE THAN I SHOULD.

...IT'S ALWAYS SUCH A PLEASURE TO SEE MY LITTLE SISTER.

BRON.

I DIDN'T HEAR YOU COME IN.

A LITTLE STARTLING WHEN A FAMILY MEMBER APPEARS UNEXPECTEDLY...

...ISN'T IT? OUR RECENT ENCOUNTER? I TOLD NO ONE.

NOT KORT. NOT FATHER.

I'M CERTAIN YOU WEREN'T MOTIVATED BY CHARITY. OR A SENSE OF JUSTICE.

REMEMBER MY WARNING. STAY OUT OF MY WAY.

IS MY DEAR SISTER THREATENING ME IN OUR OWN HOME? I'M CERTAIN THAT CAN'T BE THE CASE.

WE'VE WELCOMED A VISITOR SINCE YOU WERE LAST HERE.

ASHLEIGH, THIS IS MAI SHEN. SHE'S OFFERED HERSELF TO US AS AN ADVISOR IN THE WAR EFFORT.

I'M PLEASED TO FINALLY MEET YOU, ASHLEIGH. IT SEEMS *OTHER* DUTIES KEEP YOU AWAY FROM THE PALACE SO OFTEN.

I'M PLEASED I WAS ABLE TO RETURN. IT SEEMS MY PRESENCE MIGHT BE NEEDED HERE.

WE'LL *ALL* BE NEEDED AS THIS WAR PLAYS OUT. I LOOK FORWARD TO PROVIDING WHATEVER HELP I CAN TO THE RAVEN CAUSE.

BRON AND I HAVE BEEN WORKING TOGETHER QUITE CLOSELY.

BUT I'M SURE YOUR FIRST LOYALTY IS TO OUR FATHER, THE KING.

AS IS MINE.

HOW *IS* FATHER?

FATHER'S THE SAME. FATHER'S *FINE.*

ANXIOUS TO SEE HIS ONLY DAUGHTER AGAIN, I SUSPECT.

THEN I SHOULDN'T KEEP HIM WAITING.

NICE TO HAVE MET YOU, MAI SHEN. I'M SURE WE'LL CROSS PATHS AGAIN.

I'M SURE. I LOOK FORWARD TO IT.

DAMN!

THE *ONE* COASTAL GARRISON WE'VE YET TO REINFORCE AND *THAT'S* WHERE THEY DECIDE TO LAND.

FATHER'S GOING TO BE *SO* PLEASED.

DEET

THEY'RE HERE, FATHER. THE HERONS LANDED THEIR FORCES *HERE*. THEY'RE ALREADY OVERWHELMING US.

THE GARRISON WILL BE LOST, KORT?

YES.

WE'LL GAIN NOTHING BY THROWING AWAY LIVES IN A FUTILE ENGAGEMENT.

PULL BACK WHAT TROOPS YOU CAN, THEN GET TO YOUR MOUNT AND RETURN TO THE KEEP.

AS YOU COMMAND. FATHER...

THE HERONS STRUCK WHERE WE WERE LEAST PREPARED TO DEFEND A LANDING. AS IF THEY *KNEW.*

PERHAPS THEY DID, KING VIKTOR. IF NOTHING ELSE, THEY WERE ABLE TO PREDICT OUR WEAK LINK.

ATTACKING A FORTRESS THAT WAS APT TO BE LESS PROTECTED, EVEN THOUGH IT REPRESENTS A LESS ENTICING LANDING SITE, IS THE SAME COURSE I WOULD HAVE PURSUED.

IT'S POSSIBLE YOU'RE NOT THE *ONLY* ONES WHO HAVE OBTAINED STRATEGIC ADVICE FROM AN OUTSIDE SOURCE.

WHAT'S THE DIFFERENCE *WHERE* THEY GOT THE IDEA? NOW THEY HAVE A FOOTHOLD.

WE SHOULD HAVE INVADED THEIR SHORES AGAIN RATHER THAN WAITING FOR THEM TO COME TO US.

WE NEED TO TAKE THE WAR TO *THEM!*

OUR FIRST LANDING, AT POINT KORDAY, WAS AN UTTER DISASTER.

OR HAD YOU FORGOTTEN THE ROUT WE SUFFERED UNDER *YOUR* COMMAND?

THEY *KNEW!* THEY KNEW WHERE WE WERE GOING TO LAND AND THEY SURPRISED US!

YOU ACT AS IF THE BATTLE WAS DEVOID OF ACHIEVEMENT. I *SLEW* ONE OF THEIR PRINCES.

AND IT SERVED ONLY TO STIFFEN THE HERON RESOLVE. YOU COULD HAVE MADE A PRISONER OF HIM...

...BUT INSTEAD YOU CHOSE TO MAKE A MARTYR OF YOUR ENEMY.

I SALVAGED WHAT I COULD AND ESCAPED WITH ENOUGH OF OUR ARMY INTACT TO FIGHT ANOTHER DAY!

IS *ANYTHING* EVER GOOD ENOUGH FOR YOU?

ANYTHING?

I WON'T TOLERATE THESE OUTBURSTS IN MY WAR ROOM.

LEAVE.

AS YOU WISH.

BUT I SWEAR TO YOU, FATHER...

...THE DAY WILL COME WHEN YOU WON'T BE ABLE TO DISMISS ME SO EASILY.

REALLY? I'M SURPRISED SUCH A THING COULD HAPPEN NOW THAT WE HAVE A BRILLIANT STRATEGIC MIND IN OUR MIDST.

EVEN THOSE WHO ARE WELL-PREPARED FOR CONFLICT CAN STILL BE SURPRISED AND DEFEATED.

YOU'D DO WELL TO REMEMBER THAT.

YOU'D DO WELL TO REMEMBER YOUR ADVICE EXTENDS TO MILITARY AFFAIRS...

...NOT *FAMILY* ONES.

DO YOU UNDERSTAND ME?

THERE'S VERY LITTLE ABOUT YOU I *DON'T* UNDERSTAND. YOU'RE THE ONE WITHOUT ANY CONCEPT OF WHO YOU'RE DEALING WITH. BUT IF YOU STAY THIS COURSE...

...I *PROMISE* YOU YOU'LL FIND OUT.

OH, I INTEND TO FIND OUT.

YOU'VE KEPT MY HOUND AT YOUR SIDE LONG ENOUGH, SISTER. I WANT HIM BACK.

HERE, REAVER. COME TO ME.

REAVER, *COME!*

COME!

DAMN YOU, DOG! *COME HERE!*

I DON'T THINK HE'S LISTENING. *DESPITE* YOUR TONE.

OR PERHAPS *BECAUSE* OF IT.

ENJOY THESE PETTY VICTORIES WHILE YOU CAN, ASHLEIGH. ONE DAY THE ORDER HERE WILL CHANGE...

...AND YOU'D BE WISE TO BE CAREFUL WHEN IT DOES.

FATHER?

I CHECKED THE WAR ROOM, BUT THEY TOLD ME YOU'D ALREADY LEFT.

I THOUGHT THIS MIGHT BE THE BEST PLACE TO LOOK.

YOU KNOW ME TOO WELL, DAUGHTER.

THERE WAS NOTHING MORE TO BE ACCOMPLISHED BY STARING AT THE SAME MAP TABLES AND CALCULATING TROOP STRENGTHS YET AGAIN.

THE HERONS HAVE LANDED AND TAKEN A COASTAL GARRISON, THE ONE I'D PLACED UNDER KORT'S COMMAND.

THANKFULLY HE WAS ABLE TO AVOID CAPTURE.

OR A WORSE FATE.

I COME TO THE THRONE HALL HOPING TO DRAW INSPIRATION FROM THOSE WHO GUIDED OUR DYNASTY IN THE PAST.

PARTICULARLY WHEN IT'S OUR DYNASTY'S *FUTURE* THAT CONCERNS ME.

BECAUSE OF THE WAR?

NO.

NOT THE WAR.

WALK WITH ME.

I WAS STILL A YOUNG MAN WHEN I INHERITED THE THRONE FROM MY MOTHER. NOW MY BONES CREAK WHEN I GET OUT OF BED EACH MORNING.

I'M OLD, ASHLEIGH. NO ONE RULES FOREVER.

BRON IS THE ELDEST. HE'S TO FOLLOW ME TO THAT THRONE...

...AND HE'S NOT READY. I HAVE GRAVE DOUBTS HE EVER *WILL* BE.

THE MANTLE OF RULERSHIP DOES NOT REST EASILY ON THOSE OF HIS TEMPERAMENT.

HE'S TOO QUICK TO ANGER, TOO PRONE TO CASUAL VIOLENCE.

PERHAPS HIS NATURE IS THE PRODUCT OF HIS MOTHER NOT BEING ALIVE TO RAISE HIM. I DON'T KNOW.

GENERATIONS OF OUR FAMILY HAVE TAKEN THEIR PLACE ON THE RAVEN THRONE. SOME BETTER, SOME WORSE, BUT THE *DYNASTY* HAS ALWAYS SURVIVED.

PLEASE, *SIT*.

WHAT?

FATHER, IT'S NOT MY PLACE TO SIT UPON THE THRONE.

I WISH IT *WERE*.

IT WOULD BE...

...SAVE FOR THE SIMPLE TIMING OF YOUR BIRTH. IF ONLY YOU'D BEEN BORN FIRST, *YOU* WOULD BE IN LINE TO RULE.

THERE'S NOTHING TO BE DONE ABOUT IT, FATHER.

WHATEVER HIS FAULTS, IT'S BRON'S BIRTHRIGHT.

TRADITION DEMANDS THE ELDEST ASCENDS TO THE THRONE.

PERHAPS IT'S TIME TRADITION IS BROKEN.

YOU'RE NOT SERIOUSLY CONSIDERING SUCH A THING?

I MIGHT...

...IF I KNEW MY CHOSEN SUCCESSOR WOULD PLACE NO *OTHER* CAUSES BEFORE THOSE OF HER BLOODLINE.

OTHER CAUSES? I'M NOT SURE WHAT—

DON'T INSULT ME. DO YOU THINK I RULE AN ENTIRE KINGDOM BUT REMAIN IGNORANT OF MY OWN FAMILY'S WORKINGS?

BRON *DID* TELL YOU.

BRON TOLD ME *NOTHING*.

I'VE BEEN AWARE OF YOUR INVOLVEMENT WITH THE UNDERGROUND FOR SOME TIME. THE CLUES WERE PLAIN ENOUGH.

BUT AS LONG AS YOU DIDN'T CREATE UNDUE STRIFE WITHIN THE KINGDOM...

...I LOOKED THE OTHER WAY.

TRUE PASSION FOR A CAUSE IS AN ADMIRABLE QUALITY, ASHLEIGH. BUT YOUR PASSION IS MISPLACED.

IT'S TIME YOU PUT ASIDE THE THINGS OF YOUR WILD YOUTH AND TOOK YOUR PLACE WITH YOUR FAMILY.

IT'S POSSIBLE SOME ACCOMODATION EVENTUALLY CAN BE MADE FOR THE UNDERGROUND AND LESSER RACES.

BUT NOW YOUR LOYALTY MUST BE *HERE*.

I MUST HAVE YOUR SUPPORT IN WHAT'S AHEAD. I'VE INDULGED YOUR INDISCRETIONS AND ASKED LITTLE OF YOU IN RETURN.

NOW I ASK YOU TO PLACE YOUR DYNASTY AND YOUR KINGDOM FIRST.

WILL YOU GIVE ME YOUR LOYALTY WHEN I NEED IT?

BUT...

...BUT, FATHER, I'M...

...YES.

DEAL WITH HIM? MY FATHER IS KING. I WILL BE KING AFTER HIM. ALL I NEED DO IS *WAIT*...

...AND WHAT I WANT WILL COME TO ME.

SO *YOU* BELIEVE.

BUT YOUR FATHER BELIEVES YOU'RE NOT READY FOR THE THRONE. BELIEVES YOU NEVER WILL BE. THOSE WERE HIS *OWN* WORDS TONIGHT...

...*TO YOUR SISTER.*

THEY'RE CONSPIRING TO BREACH THE ORDER OF SUCCESSION AND PUT ASHLEIGH ON THE THRONE IN YOUR PLACE.

BUT... ...THE FIRST BORN HAS *ALWAYS* INHERITED THE THRONE. EVEN MY FATHER WOULDN'T CONSIDER SUCH A BREAK WITH TRADITION.

HOW COULD YOU *POSSIBLY* KNOW ANY OF THIS?

YOU KNOW BETTER THAN TO DOUBT ME.

WHY WOULD HE BETRAY ME SO?!

WHAT MORE MUST I *DO?!*

THE GARRISON WE LOST? WHAT DO YOU EXPECT WITH PRINCE KORT IN CHARGE? HE'S EVEN-HANDED FOR A ROYAL, BUT...

BUT HE'S NO SOLDIER.

DAMN THIS WEATHER.

IT'S THE CAPTAIN'S FAULT. I WASN'T EVEN *SUPPOSED* TO BE WALKING PERIMETER TONIGHT, BUT AS SOON AS THE SKY OPENS UP, *I* GET SENT OUT HERE TO BE SOAKED TO THE SKIN.

I'M TELLING YOU, CAPTAIN'S GOT IT IN FOR ME.

STOP COMPLAINING.

WOULD YOU RATHER BE POSTED TO THE FRONT LINES DEFENDING THE COAST AGAINST THE HERONS?

WHEN YOU PUT IT THAT WAY...

YOU HEARD ABOUT THE LANDING?

NO, HE'S NO SOLDIER. SAY WHAT YOU WANT ABOUT PRINCE BRON, BUT I'D RATHER HAVE *HIM* AT MY BACK THAN HIS BROTHER WHEN SWORDS ARE DRAWN.

I HEAR THE HERONS ARE HUNKERED DOWN IN THE FORTRESS THEY TOOK, WAITING FOR REINFORCEMENTS BEFORE THEY TRY TO ADVANCE.

THE COAST IS AS FAR AS THEY'LL GET. I GUARANTEE YOU...

...OUR **DYNASTY'S** FUTURE. I GROW CONCERNED FOR THIS KINGDOM OUR FAMILY HAS BUILT. I WANT TO BE CERTAIN ALL WE HAVE ACHIEVED WILL **CONTINUE** WHEN I AM NO MORE.

I'M SURE THESE ARE THOUGHTS **YOU** SHARE, BRON.

THE WEIGHT OF HISTORY IS A HEAVY THING, FATHER.

WE TRACE OUR LINEAGE IN A DIRECT LINE, AN UNBROKEN SUCCESSION FROM PARENT TO ELDEST CHILD DATING BACK CENTURIES.

IT'S **ALWAYS** BEEN SO.

I HAVE KNOWN FROM THE TIME I WAS A CHILD THAT THE RESPONSIBILITY FOR THE THRONE, FOR THE FUTURE OF THE RAVEN DYNASTY, WOULD BE MINE.

IT IS MY **BIRTHRIGHT.**

I HELD THAT KNOWLEDGE CLOSE AND PREPARED MYSELF FOR IT EVERY DAY OF MY LIFE.

AND YET YOU WOULD PLACE **ASHLEIGH** ON THE THRONE RATHER THAN ME.

145

SO. THE WALLS TRULY DO HAVE EARS.

WHY WOULD YOU DO THIS TO ME, FATHER?

BECAUSE THE RESPONSIBILITY OF TRUE POWER IS FAR DIFFERENT THAN THE SIMPLE EXERCISE OF AUTHORITY.

THE THRONE BELONGS TO THE FIRST BORN.

I *WILL* CLAIM IT.

YOU CAN'T MANAGE TO CONTROL *YOURSELF*...

...HOW DO YOU THINK YOU COULD EVER CONTROL AN ENTIRE EMPIRE?

YOU'RE NO MORE PREPARED TO LEAD THIS KINGDOM THAN IS THAT DAMN HOUND OF YOURS.

AND YOU GIVE ME NO SIGN YOU EVER *WILL* BE.

CRUELTY FOR ITS OWN SAKE AND FITS OF TEMPER DON'T BEFIT A MONARCH.

IF TRADITION DEMANDS I PLACE MY KINGDOM IN THE HANDS OF A PETULANT CHILD, THEN TRADITION BE DAMNED.

I WON'T ALLOW THE MERE TIMING OF YOUR SISTER'S BIRTH TO PREVENT THE FITTEST RULER FROM FOLLOWING ME TO THE RAVEN THRONE.

I'M SORRY, FATHER...

FATHER?
I REALIZE
IT'S LATE,
BUT...

OR WAS IT SOMEONE *ELSE* CLOSE TO THE KING WHO COMMITTED THIS HEINOUS ACT?

SOMEONE WITH AN *OBVIOUS* MOTIVE.

WHAT...

...HAVE YOU BECOME?

I'VE BECOME *KING*.

BUT AT SUCH A *BITTER* PRICE. MY FATHER MURDERED, AND THE CRIME PERPETRATED BY MY OWN *SISTER*.

SHOCKING TO THINK HER MISGUIDED LOYALTY TO THE UNDERGROUND LED HER TO *SLAY* HER OWN FATHER IN AN ATTEMPT TO TAKE POWER.

AND IF I HADN'T BEEN ABLE TO OVERCOME HER, THE DEATHS OF HER BROTHERS WERE SURELY NEXT.

I'LL BLAME MYSELF, OF COURSE. I'LL CARRY THE BURDEN OF GUILT FOR NOT RECOGNIZING THE VIPER IN OUR MIDST UNTIL TOO LATE.

SUCH A TRAGEDY. WHEN I ASCEND TO THE RAVEN THRONE, MY FIRST DUTIES WILL BE TO ATTEND TO MY FATHER'S FUNERAL...

...AND MY SISTER'S EXECUTION.

YOU'RE *MAD*. YOU ACTUALLY BELIEVE YOU CAN GET AWAY WITH THIS.

WHEN WILL *I* BE ABLE TO DO THAT?

YOU ALREADY *CAN.* THAT AND *MORE.*

I'VE *GIVEN* YOU THE POWER, ALL YOU NEED DO IS LEARN TO HARNESS IT.

AND I'M A *VERY* GOOD TEACHER.

I ALWAYS INTENDED TO SHIFT THE BLAME TO ASHLEIGH. HER WALKING IN MADE IT THAT MUCH EASIER.

I'LL SUMMON THE GUARDS AND HAVE HER TAKEN TO THE DUNGEONS.

WHAT OF YOUR BROTHER?

WILL HE PRESENT ANY DIFFICULTIES?

KORT'S NEVER BEEN TERRIBLY CLEVER. HE'LL BELIEVE WHATEVER I TELL HIM.

HE'S ALWAYS BEEN TERRIFIED SOMETHING WOULD HAPPEN TO ME. HE'S NEVER WANTED THE THRONE HIMSELF.

KORT WILL BE A BOON IN ALL THIS.

SEND HIM HERE BUT TELL HIM NOTHING. I WANT HIM TO HEAR OF HIS SISTER'S TREACHERY FROM HIS DEAR BROTHER'S LIPS. NO...

...IN FACT, SEND HIM TO THE THRONE ROOM.

WHERE ELSE WOULD THE KING BE?

THE UNDERGROUND. HER INVOLVEMENT WITH THEM SHOULD COME AS NO SURPRISE. IT'S WHY SHE WAS CONSTANTLY ABSENT FROM THE KEEP...

...AND WHY SHE KILLED FATHER.

I EXPECT *YOU* WERE HER NEXT TARGET. THEN SHE WOULD HAVE FRAMED ME FOR BOTH MURDERS AND TAKEN THE THRONE FOR HERSELF.

ASHLEIGH...

YES, *ASHLEIGH*. ALL SO SHE COULD FURTHER THE INSANE CAUSE OF THOSE LESSER RACE VERMIN.

AT LEAST SHE WAS FOUND OUT BEFORE ALL OF HER PLAN COULD COME TO FRUITION.

I'M KING NOW. AND THIS WON'T GO UNPUNISHED. ASHLEIGH IS ALREADY CONFINED WITHIN THE DUNGEON. *HER* FATE IS A FOREGONE CONCLUSION.

...AS A *SHOW* OF RAVEN STRENGTH.

YOU SAVED MY LIFE ON THE BATTLEFIELD OF POINT KORDAY. NOW I NEED YOU AGAIN, KORT.

TAKE A CONTINGENT OF OUR TROOPS, FIND THE SANCTUARY, AND RAZE IT TO THE GROUND.

WILL YOU DO THIS FOR ME, BROTHER?

BUT THE UNDERGROUND ITSELF MUST PAY. THEIR SANCTUARY IS IN THE NORTH, SOMEWHERE NEAR THE RUINS TO WHICH WE TRACKED MY ESCAPED SLAVE.

I WANT THE SANCTUARY *DESTROYED* AS PUNISHMENT...

I AM YOUR SERVANT, MY KING.

SKRAKOOM

GETTING INSIDE THE KEEP AND KNOWING WHERE WE ARE IS WELL AND GOOD, BUT WE NEED TO KNOW WHERE WE'RE *GOING*.

WE HAVE ONLY A FEW HOURS BEFORE DAWN AND THIS PLACE IS TOO VAST FOR US TO WANDER UNTIL WE SIMPLY STUMBLE ACROSS BRON.

I THINK *THAT'S* THE ONE. THAT'S WHERE THEY HAD US...

OR WORSE, UNTIL *HE* STUMBLES ACROSS *US*.

...BEFORE...

ETHAN, WHAT ARE YOU DOING? YOU'LL GIVE US AWAY!

WE DON'T HAVE *TIME* FOR THIS!

WE *HAVE* TO...

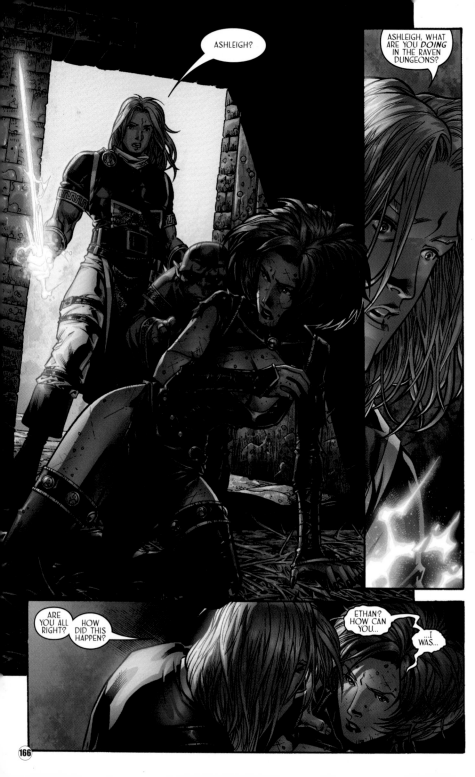

BRON.

BRON PUT ME IN HERE.

AFTER HE KILLED THE KING.

AFTER...

...WHAT?

BRON *KILLED* KING VIKTOR?

I CAME HERE INTENDING TO KILL *BRON*, TO TAKE VENGEANCE FOR MY BROTHER'S MURDER AT POINT KORDAY.

AND YOU'RE SAYING HE'S MURDERED HIS OWN FATHER? THERE'S NO *END* TO HIS CARNAGE, IS THERE?

OBVIOUSLY YOU WEREN'T THERE.

I HAVEN'T BEEN AT THE SANCTUARY IN A WHILE. I...

I WAS HOPING YOU'D BE ABLE TO LEAD ME TO BRON. I WENT TO THE UNDERGROUND'S SANCTUARY LOOKING FOR YOU.

...NEEDED TO BE HERE AT THE KEEP.

ETHAN, THERE'S SOMETHING I SHOULD TELL YOU ABOUT BRON...

WE HAVE COMPANY.

THANKS...

...BUT I *COULD* HAVE HANDLED HIM MYSELF.

YOU'RE WELCOME.

AND I *REALIZE* YOU COULD'VE HANDLED HIM YOURSELF...

...SEEING AS YOU'RE APPARENTLY NEVER *UNARMED.* THAT'S SOMETHING TO DO WITH THAT *MARK* ON YOUR ARM YOU WERE GOING ON ABOUT?

IT IS.

I'M STILL LEARNING EXACTLY WHAT IT DOES, BUT THIS IS PART OF IT.

SKINK, ARE YOU OKAY?

I WILL BE.

SEEMS LIKE SOMEONE'S ALWAYS KNOCKING YOU OUT OF THE WAY TO GET TO ME.

SORRY.

IT'S ALL RIGHT, ETHAN. IT'S PRETTY HARD TO REALLY HURT ME.

COME ON, WE NEED TO BE GONE BEFORE MORE GUARDS SHOW UP.

MAYBE YOU CAN STILL LEAD ME TO BRON IF YOU KNOW WHERE HE IS.

PROBABLY THE THRONE ROOM, BUT...

ETHAN, *WAIT.*

YOUR BROTHER CUT **MY** BROTHER'S THROAT!

ALL THIS TIME, AND YOU DIDN'T SAY **ANYTHING**.

WHAT DID YOU **WANT** ME TO DO? HANG A SIGN AROUND MY NECK?

I SHOULD HAVE KNOWN.

THE WAY YOU GOT IN AND OUT OF THE KEEP, SEEING YOU ON THE BATTLEFIELD, THE REACTION TO YOUR NAME AT THE SANCTUARY.

EVEN THE **DOG**.

IT ALL MAKES SENSE...

...BECAUSE YOU'RE **ONE** OF THEM.

YOU SAY *"ONE OF THEM"* LIKE IT'S A CRIME.

YOU WANT ME TO BE ASHAMED OF BEING PART OF THE RAVEN DYNASTY? I'M **NOT**.

YOU DIDN'T KNOW WHO I WAS BECAUSE I'M THE YOUNGEST CHILD. WE'RE **TRADITIONALLY** KEPT OUT OF THE PUBLIC EYE.

BUT MY HERITAGE DOESN'T CHANGE MY LOYALTY TO THE UNDERGROUND. IT DOESN'T CHANGE WHO I **AM**.

THIS CHANGES EVERYTHING.

TO THINK I WAS ACTUALLY...

WHAT?

NOTHING.

I CAME HERE TO KILL BRON. THAT'S WHAT I INTEND TO DO.

WITH OR WITHOUT YOUR HELP.

BUT...

...I...

WELL?

THAT'S WHAT I THOUGHT.

ETHAN? ARE YOU SURE THIS IS WHAT YOU WANT TO DO?

THIS IS WHAT I *SWORE* I WOULD DO.

IT'S STILL THE EARLY MORNING...

...BRON'S GOING TO BE *DEAD* BEFORE MOST OF THE KEEP IS EVEN AWAKE.

FIRST THE CORONATION...

...SO THERE'S NO DOUBT IN THE PEOPLE'S MINDS AS TO WHO THEIR MONARCH IS.

THEN FATHER'S FUNERAL WITH THE PROPER POMP AND OUTPOURING OF GRIEF, SO THE PEOPLE SEE I'M COMPASSIONATE.

AND FINALLY ASHLEIGH'S EXECUTION, SO THEY'RE REMINDED I CAN BE UNFORGIVING WHEN NECESSARY.

MAI SHEN, HAS MY BROTHER LEFT TO UNDERTAKE THE TASK I LAID BEFORE HIM?

KORT'S ALREADY GONE.

EVERYTHING WE'VE SET IN MOTION IS COMING TO—

BRON!

SO YOU DELIVER YOURSELF TO ME, ETHAN.

I DON'T KNOW WHETHER TO BE IMPRESSED YOU MADE IT THIS FAR, OR AMUSED THAT YOU'RE FOOLHARDY ENOUGH TO CHALLENGE ME AT THE VERY HEART OF MY POWER.

KILLING MY BROTHER WASN'T ENOUGH FOR YOU, BUTCHER?

YOU HAD TO MURDER YOUR *OWN FATHER* AS WELL?

MY FATHER?

I'M AFRAID YOU'RE MISINFORMED. THE TRUTH, AS TERRIBLE AS IT MAY BE, IS THAT MY *SISTER* WAS RESPONSIBLE FOR THE KING'S DEATH.

SO TRAGIC WHEN A SIBLING GOES BAD...

...THOUGH I SUPPOSE IN YOUR CASE YOU HAVE *ONE LESS* TO WORRY ABOUT.

ALMOST AS TRAGIC AS THE DEATH OF AN HEIR TO THE THRONE.

YES, WELL...

...*I'M* HEIR NO LONGER.

THE THRONE AND ALL ITS RESPONSIBILITIES HAVE PASSED TO ME.

FITTING, DON'T YOU THINK, FOR ME TO START MY REIGN BY KILLING *YOU?*

THAT'S IRONIC.

I THOUGHT I'D *END* YOUR REIGN BY KILLING *YOU.*

TRY.

Oh, YES...

...I THINK YOU *ARE* SURPRISED.

SKUH...

...SKINK?

I THINK... I MIGHT BE...

...hhhhh

ETHAN!

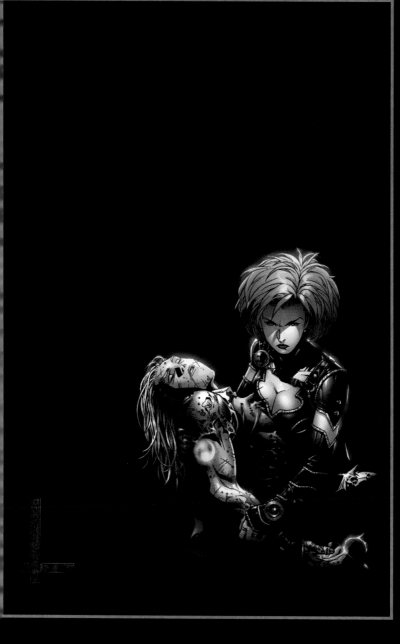

I CAN'T BREAK MYSELF OF THINKING HE'LL BE THERE.

I'LL HEAR A FOOTFALL BEHIND ME, OR SEE A SHADOW ON THE WALL, AND I'LL TURN AND EXPECT TO SEE ARTOR THERE SMILING AT ME.

BUT HE NEVER IS.

I'M NOT SURE WHICH IS WORSE, DANE— HAVING BURIED OUR OLDEST SON...

...OR NOT KNOWING IF WE'LL HAVE TO DO THE SAME FOR OUR YOUNGEST.

ETHAN'S ABSENCE WEIGHS UPON ME AS WELL, MARIELLA.

BUT NO AMOUNT OF DISCUSSION COULD CONVINCE HIM HE WAS SIMPLY A CONVENIENT TRIGGER AND NOT THE *CAUSE* OF THIS CONFLICT.

WE'LL BURY FAR TOO MANY OF THIS KINGDOM'S SONS AND DAUGHTERS BEFORE OUR WAR WITH THE RAVENS IS DONE.

I PRAY ETHAN IS NOT AMONG THEM.

VIKTOR HAD LONG STOKED THE FIRES OF WAR. NOW THAT HE'S FANNED THOSE FLAMES TO LIFE...

DIED? *HOW?*

WHAT'S HAPPENED?

THE DETAILS AREN'T COMPLETELY CLEAR, BUT WE KNOW THE KING IS DEAD.

THE YOUNGEST CHILD IS RUMORED RESPONSIBLE.

REGICIDE.

VIKTOR FORCED THIS WAR, BUT I WOULD NOT HAVE WISHED THIS FATE UPON HIM.

THE THRONE BELONGS TO THE ELDEST NOW? TO *BRON?*

AYE, FATHER.

THE MAN WHO *MURDERED* ARTOR NOW SITS UPON THE RAVEN THRONE.

THIS BODES ILL FOR THE WAR.

HOW SO? WON'T THIS THROW THE RAVENS INTO A DISARRAY THAT WILL BE TO OUR ADVANTAGE?

I *KNEW* VIKTOR. I COULD PREDICT HIM.

AT *BEST* BRON IS A WILD CARD. AT WORST HE COULD BE A MADMAN.

AND ETHAN WENT TO THE EAST VOWING TO SLAY HIM.

IT GIVES ME NO COMFORT KNOWING *YLENA* IS IN THE EAST AS WELL, BUT AT LEAST SHE'S SECURE BEHIND THE WALLS OF THE FORTRESS SHE AND HER TROOPS TOOK.

WITH ETHAN...

...WE HAVE NO WAY OF KNOWING IF HE'S EVEN *ALIVE.*

I WANT THIS PIECE OF MEAT REMOVED FROM MY THRONE HALL...

...AND HAVE THAT HUMPBACKED FREAK EXECUTED AS WELL.

COME ALONG.

I WON'T LET THIS END LIKE—

YOU WEREN'T SATISFIED WITH FATHER...

UF!

...AND AVENGE FATHER ANOTHER DAY.

MY FIRST INSTINCT WAS TO ESCAPE...

BUT I'M GLAD I THOUGHT BETTER OF IT.

FOR *EVERYTHING* YOU'VE DONE, BROTHER...

...YOU *DESERVE* TO DIE!

AHHH!

DO YOU HAVE *ANY* IDEA WHAT I CAN DO?!

ANY?!

194

"...NO ONE WILL DARE TAKE THEM IN."

GHUK

KOFF

KOFF KOFF

...YOU *WERE* SERIOUS.

NO TIME... *KOFF*

...NO TIME TO REST. WE HAVE TO GET MOVING.

MOVING *WHERE?*

WE'RE FUGITIVES IN THE MIDDLE OF THE RAVEN CAPITAL.

I THINK WE'RE A LITTLE TOO CONSPICUOUS TO BLEND IN WITH THE CROWD.

I *KNOW* PEOPLE.

RUDD!

WE NEED YOUR HELP.

ASHLEIGH?

I WASN'T *EXPECTING* YOU...

TO WHAT DO I OWE THE SURPRISE?

I DON'T HAVE MUCH TIME TO EXPLAIN, RUDD, BUT BRON'S MURDERED MY FATHER AND TAKEN THE THRONE.

HE'S BLAMING *ME* FOR THE CRIME. HE WOULD'VE HAD ME EXECUTED IF I HADN'T ESCAPED.

I KNOW YOUR BROTHER'S A BAD SEED, BUT *THIS*...

I DAMN *MYSELF* FOR NOT SEEING IT IN TIME.

RUDD, WE NEED TO BE OUT OF THE CITY AND ON OUR WAY TO THE SANCTUARY.

YOUR FRIEND CAN BE TRUSTED?

HE'S EVEN MORE OF A FUGITIVE THAN I AM.

ETHAN, THIS IS RUDD. THE UNDERGROUND HAS SUPPORTERS *OTHER* THAN ME.

THAT'S A *RECOGNIZABLE* FACE YOU WEAR, PRINCE.

YOU'RE LUCKY YOU FELL IN WITH ASHLEIGH.

DEET

WHERE DOES IT LEAD?

IT'LL TAKE YOU OUT TO THE BARRENS BEYOND THE CITY WALLS.

WHIRRRRRRRRR

MORE THAN A FEW LESSER RACE SLAVES HAVE USED IT TO LEAVE THEIR CHAINS BEHIND.

THERE ARE LANTERNS AND FOOD WAITING DOWN THERE.

THANK YOU, RUDD.

ANYTHING FOR YOU, ASHLEIGH. YOU KNOW THAT.

GET YOURSELVES MOVING RIGHT AWAY. AND *BE CAREFUL.*

YOUR BROTHER'S GOING TO TEAR APART THIS CITY LOOKING FOR YOU.

YOU BE CAREFUL, TOO.

BRON'S HANDS DON'T NEED ANY *MORE* BLOOD ON THEM.

IT'S NOT *MY* BLOOD HE WANTS.

THANK YOU, FOR HELPING US.

YOU THANK ME BY TAKING CARE OF ASHLEIGH.

WATCH YOUR STEP, SKINK. THE STAIRS ARE A LITTLE SLICK.

THIS IS HOW YOU USUALLY GET OUT OF THE CITY?

ONE OF THE WAYS.

HOW LONG WILL IT TAKE US TO GET BEYOND THE WALLS?

WHIRRRRRRRRR

ONLY A FEW HOURS. THE TUNNEL RUNS IN A FAIRLY STRAIGHT LINE.

BEFORE WE GO, I NEED TO ASK YOU ABOUT THE POWER YOUR BROTHER HAD.

DO YOU KNOW HOW HE—

WHUH-WHAT'RE YOU DOING?!

WAIT. BACK IN THE KEEP, IN THE THRONE HALL, WHAT MADE YOU COME BACK?

I'M... NOT SURE.

TO SEE IF YOU WERE STILL ALIVE.

TO SEE IF BRON WAS DEAD.

I COULDN'T BRING MYSELF TO GO WITH YOU WHEN YOU ASKED ME...

...BUT I COULDN'T BRING MYSELF TO JUST WALK AWAY EITHER.

I'M GLAD YOU'RE NOT DEAD.

THANKS.

WE'RE *BOTH* WANTED NOW. BRON WON'T REST UNTIL HE HAS US.

THE ONLY SAFE PLACE WE CAN GO IS THE SANCTUARY. I ASKED YOU TO JOIN ME ONCE BEFORE...

...THE SITUATION'S NOT MUCH DIFFERENT NOW.

THE ONLY REASON I CAME HERE AGAIN WAS TO AVENGE ARTOR'S DEATH BY KILLING YOUR BROTHER.

AFTER THAT I INTENDED TO RETURN TO THE WEST, TO MY FAMILY, AND HELP WITH THE WAR.

I'M GOING NORTH TO THE SANCTUARY. DO WHATEVER YOU WANT AFTERWARD, BUT I COULD USE YOUR HELP GETTING THERE.

AND WHETHER I'M PART OF THE RAVEN DYNASTY OR NOT, YOU NEED *MY* HELP OR YOU'RE NEVER GOING TO GET OUT OF THE CITY...

...MUCH LESS ACROSS THE GREAT SEA AND HOME AGAIN. SO...

...ARE YOU COMING WITH ME OR NOT?

...NO, I *DON'T* KNOW WHERE HIS POWER CAME FROM, THOUGH I'M SURE MAI SHEN IS INVOLVED.

NEITHER OF US IS READY TO TAKE HIM ON UNTIL WE UNDERSTAND WHAT HE'S BECOME.

THAT'S NOT GOING TO HAPPEN, IS IT? YOU'LL NEVER GET CLOSE ENOUGH TO BRON, NOT NOW. EVEN IF YOU *COULD*...

SKINK? IS THIS OKAY WITH YOU?

I GO WHERE YOU GO, ETHAN.

I TRUTHFULLY DON'T THINK WE HAVE MUCH CHOICE.

ALL RIGHT, AS FAR AS THE SANCTUARY...

...BUT THEN I GO HOME.